THE RIDDLE OF THE CAMEL RACE

Nicolas Brasch  Daron Parton

Australia • Brazil • Japan • Korea • Mexico • Singapore • Spain • United Kingdom • United States

The Riddle of the Camel Race

Fast Forward
Gold Level 21

Text: Nicolas Brasch
Illustrations: Daron Parton
Editor: Johanna Rohan
Design: Vonda Pestana
Series design: James Lowe
Production controller: Seona Galbally
Audio recordings: Juliet Hill, Picture Start
Spoken by: Matthew King and Abbe Holmes
Reprint: Jennifer Foo

ISBN 978 0 17 012673 1
ISBN 978 0 17 012669 4 (set)

Cengage Learning Australia
Level 7, 80 Dorcas Street
South Melbourne, Victoria Australia 3205
Phone: 1300 790 853

Cengage Learning New Zealand
Unit 4B Rosedale Office Park
331 Rosedale Road, Albany, North Shore NZ 0632
Phone: 0508 635 766

For learning solutions, visit cengage.com.au

Printed in Australia by Ligare Pty Ltd
7 8 9 10 11 12 13 21 20 19 18 17

Evaluated in independent research by staff from the Department of Language, Literacy and Arts Education at the University of Melbourne.

THE RIDDLE OF THE CAMEL RACE

Nicolas Brasch

Daron Parton

Contents

Chapter 1 The Iron-fisted Sultan 4
Chapter 2 The Sultan's Challenge 10
Chapter 3 Off and Racing 16
Chapter 4 Shiraz to the Rescue 20

Chapter 1

THE IRON-FISTED SULTAN

Once upon a time, in a land so far away
that it could only be reached
by a supersonic jet
(although, of course, supersonic jets
didn't exist back then),
there lived a very cruel sultan.

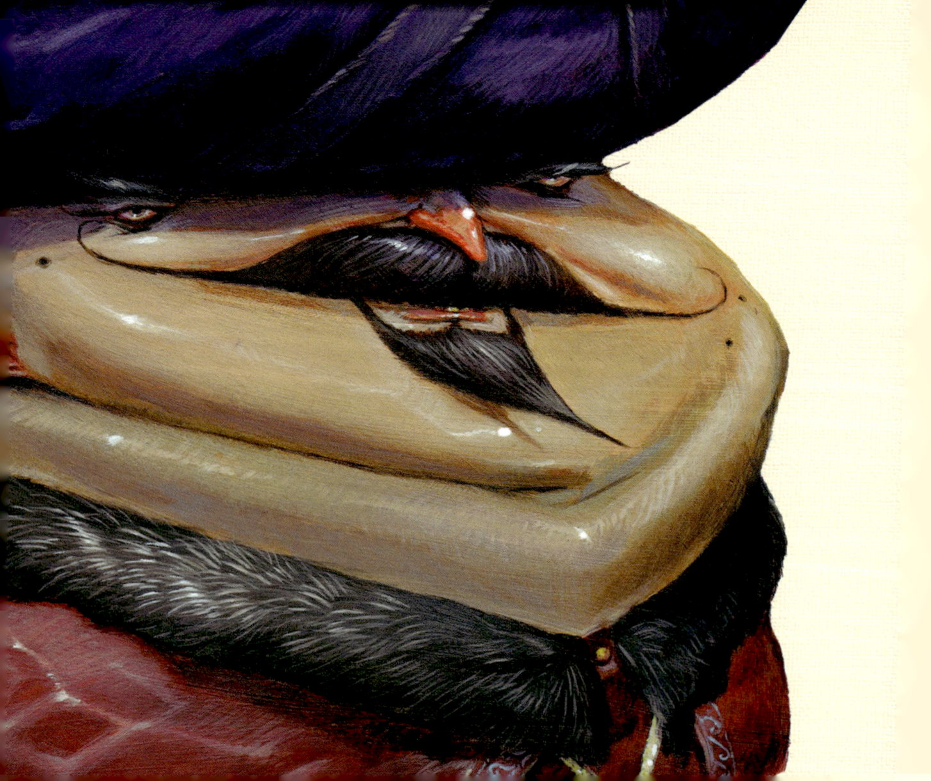

This sultan ruled his kingdom with an iron fist.

It really *was* an iron fist, because he had lost one hand in a sword fight and had ordered the best doctor in the kingdom to fit him with an iron hand.

Everyone in the land did exactly
what the sultan ordered.
They were too afraid not to.
The kingdom's prisons
were full of subjects
who had *not* done exactly
what the sultan had ordered
or had not done it fast enough.

NO VACANCIES
CAMEL RANK

For most of the year,
the sultan ordered his people
to do normal kingdom-type jobs –
guarding his castle,
hunting for his food,
cleaning his silver
and clipping his toenails.

But, once a year, on his birthday,
the sultan had a bit of fun.
He set a challenge for some
of his subjects.
No one turned down the challenge
because to do so meant many years
in prison – or worse …

THE SULTAN'S CHALLENGE

As the sultan's next birthday approached, everyone in the kingdom started getting scared.
On the morning of his birthday, they stayed in bed with their heads under their blankets –
too scared to get up and face the day.

Running Words 223

Luckily, most people had nothing to
worry about.
But two of the sultan's subjects,
Ali and Baboo,
had a lot to worry about –
for they were told to go before
the sultan.

"My challenge for you two,"
roared the sultan to the shaking duo,
"is a camel race."
The sultan stopped talking
for a moment,
to let what he had said sink in.

That doesn't sound too bad,
they both thought,
although they didn't say so,
lest the sultan made the challenge
harder.

The sultan knew that Ali and Baboo would like what they had heard. But, he wasn't getting soft in his old age. There was something he hadn't told them.

Just as Ali and Baboo started to
feel good, the sultan started
talking again.
"The winner of the race
is the person whose camel comes last!"
he told them,
with a huge grin on his face.
"The loser will get five years in prison
and a tattoo of me on his chest
to remind him of his failure."

Chapter 3

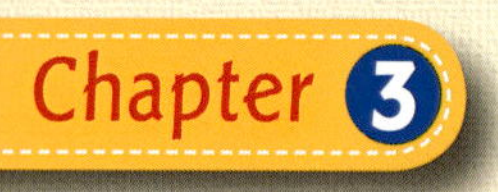

OFF AND RACING

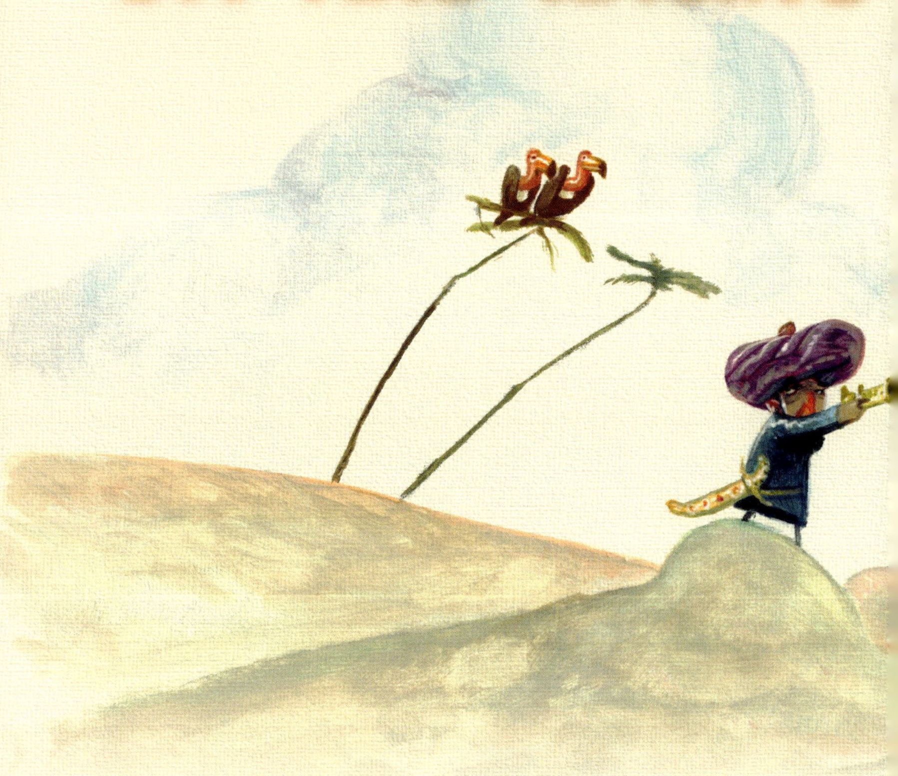

Ali and Baboo were led to the starting line of the race by two of the sultan's guards.

They were helped onto their camels and given a map of the route.

"Do not think of taking another route
so that you lose the race,"
one of the guards told them.
"If one of you does so,
you will both be sent to prison."

When Ali and Baboo were ready,
they were given the signal to set off.
They did so,
but very, very slowly.
Neither man wanted to get ahead
of the other.

Ali and Baboo were going so slowly that
before long their camels stopped.
The men looked at each other
and shook their heads.
They did not know what to do.
They knew they had to finish the race
or else they would be in trouble.
But, neither of them wanted to finish
first.

SHIRAZ TO THE RESCUE

The kingdom's wisest person,
a woman named Shiraz,
approached the men.
She gestured for them to get off
their camels, and they did.
Then, she whispered something
in each man's ear.

As soon as Shiraz had
finished speaking,
each man leapt on a camel
and dug his heels into the animal.

The camels took off,
and the men urged them on –
faster and faster.
They raced towards the finish line
as quickly as they could.
Each man was anxious
to get to the finish line first.

Those who were watching the race
were surprised at what they
were seeing –
for they knew that the winner
was the person whose camel
finished last.

One man could not stand
the tension.
He had to know why Ali and Baboo
were so anxious
to get to the finish line first.

The man approached Shiraz and asked her what she had told the camel riders.

"Simple," Shiraz said. "I just told each of them to get on the other man's camel. After all, the winner is the person whose camel comes last."